Allegra's Window

# First Day at Day Care

### Ellen Weiss
### Pictures by Nate Evans

## Aladdin Paperbacks

Aladdin Paperbacks
An imprint of Simon & Schuster Children's Publishing Division
1230 Avenue of the Americas
New York, New York 10020

First Aladdin Paperbacks edition, April 1996
Designed by Chani Yammer and Nancy Widdows
The text of this book was set in 17 point Syntax.
Manufactured in the United States of America
10 9 8 7 6 5 4 3 2 1
ISBN: 0-689-80400-8

Hi. My name is Allegra, and today is my very first, number one, never-before day of day care.

I'm really excited! But I'm a little scared, too. I wish Daddy and my brother, Rondo, could stay with me.

Here's what I'm scared of: I'm scared I won't know any of the children, and I'll be different from them, and nobody will be my friend.

I'm scared they'll play games I've never heard of.

I'm scared that they'll have yucky food to eat at snacktime, like zootabaga stew with zootabaga sauce on top.

I'm scared maybe I'll have to share.
Sometimes I don't like to share. For instance,
I will *not* share Godfrey, my stuffed octopus.

And I'm scared I'll have to take a nap, and nobody will rub my back. Mommy *always* rubs my back before I fall asleep.

I'm scared it will be dark . . .

and I'm scared there might even be *monsters*!

Here comes Ms. Melody. She seems really nice. She gives me an elephant sticker.

Ms. Melody introduces me to Laurie, and we play in the block corner together. And then we're friends . . . just like that.

The first game everyone plays is Duck Duck Goose. Rondo taught me that game last year!

For snack, there's peanut butter on crackers and some raisins . . . and not one single zootabaga!

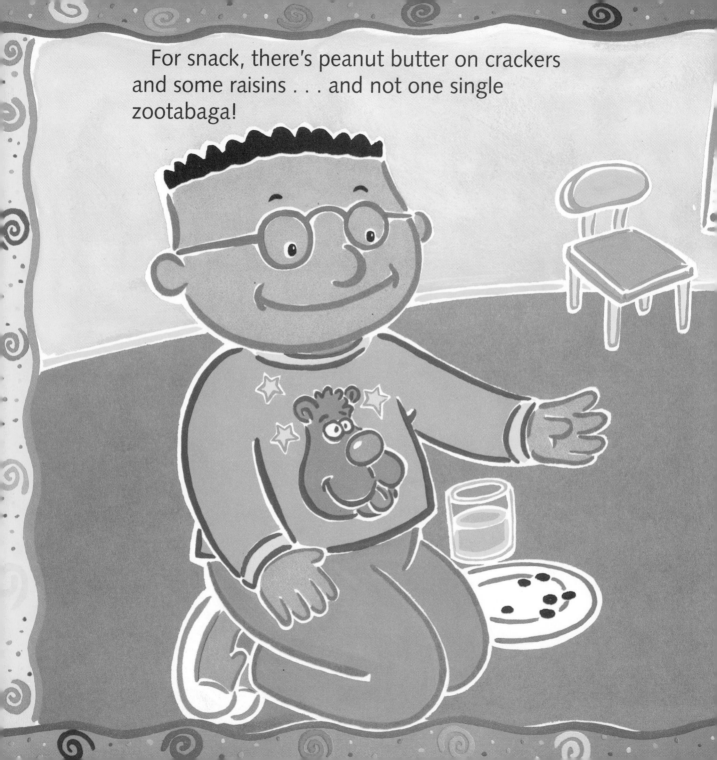

Micah shares his raisins with me, and I share
my peanut butter with him. I don't have to
share Godfrey at all if I don't feel like it.

Ms. Melody rubs my back when we lie down for naptime. It's not very dark at all.

And when we get up, we cut . . . and draw . . .
and color . . . and glue . . . .

And guess what? There *are* monsters at day care . . .

But I'm one of them!
See you tomorrow, Ms. Melody!